RAISE THE
STAKES

THE CONTEST
00:00:03

RAISE THE STAKES

Megan Atwood

darbycreek

MINNEAPOLIS

Darby Creek
A division of Lerner Publishing Group, Inc.
241 First Avenue North
Minneapolis, MN 55401 USA

For reading levels and more information, look up this title at
www.lernerbooks.com.

The images in this book are used with the permission of: © g-stockstudio/Shutterstock.com (teen male); © Andycash/Dreamstime.com (digital clock); © Vidakovic/Bigstock.com (Abstract technology background); © iStockphoto.com/archibald1221 (circle background): © freesoulproduction/Shutterstock.com (game pieces).

Main body text set in Janson Text LT Std 12/17.5.
Typeface provided by Adobe Systems.

Library of Congress Cataloging-in-Publication Data

The Cataloging-in-Publication Data for *Raise the Stakes* is on file at the Library of Congress.
ISBN 978-1-4677-7508-3 (lib. bdg.)
ISBN 978-1-4677-8103-9 (pbk.)
ISBN 978-1-4677-8833-5 (EB pdf)

Manufactured in the United States of America
1 – SB – 12/31/15

To my parents, always.

CHAPTER 1

Colin's palms were sweating, like they always did when he was nervous. And he'd been nervous a lot lately.

But it was too late now. He'd signed up for the Contest. He'd already done two tasks—two weird, kind of intrusive tasks. And the Benefactor—whoever was running this competition—expected Colin to follow through on Task 3.

Colin swallowed and pushed on the revolving door. His next task was to go into a business he'd never heard of, pretend to be someone he wasn't, complain about something he didn't understand, and plant a bug under someone's desk.

Man, his palms were sweaty.

At the front desk, two bored security guards eyed him, and one said, "Can I help you?"

"Uh . . ." Colin wiped his hands on his khakis—his best pair. His only pair. "I need to go to SolarStar."

The guard went back to reading. "Fifteenth floor."

Colin nodded and then walked to the elevators. It was two o'clock on a Monday afternoon. The place was pretty empty. He adjusted the tie clip on his dad's old tie. The clip also happened to be a camera. Transmitting to someone, somewhere, for some reason. He felt the listening device in his pocket. He assumed it was already recording, just like the camera. But it was Colin's job to plant it inside SolarStar. The Benefactor's instructions repeated in his head: *Put the device in Len Steinberg's office, under his desk directly beneath the phone.* He'd never had to spy on anyone before, but he suspected this was going to be his hardest task so far. The other two tasks had been weird and uncomfortable, but he hadn't

needed to actually talk to anyone when he
did them.

And this one felt extra creepy, because it
meant that the Benefactor knew certain things
about Colin.

1. He looked older than his seventeen years.
2. He could look and sound intimidating.
   And of course . . .
3. He needed the money. Bad.

* * * * *

Standing in front of SolarStar's reception desk,
Colin put on his mad face. He knew how to
look like someone you wouldn't want to mess
with. His parents owned a business—well, his
mom owned it, now that his dad was gone—
and Colin worked evenings at the family
hardware store. He'd seen his share of angry
customers. People who thought they had a
right to complain, even if complaining wouldn't
change anything. He figured he could pull off
that attitude.

"I need to talk to Len Steinberg.
Immediately."

The receptionist's eyes got wide. "One moment, sir."

Colin pushed down the inclination to say, "It's OK."

"Um, Mr. Steinberg, I have a . . ." the receptionist looked at Colin expectantly.

Colin said, "Ray Johnson." That was the name the Benefactor had told him to use. "I own stock in this company, and I have a complaint."

". . . a Mr. Johnson here who needs assistance. He seems unhappy." The receptionist hung up the phone and put on a broad smile for Colin. "He'll be right with you, sir."

Colin kept the scowl on his face. "I certainly hope so."

His instructions specifically said he needed to get a good look at this whole floor, on top of bugging an office. The Benefactor had given him a script for what to say to Mr. Steinberg too. Colin had it memorized. As he paced around the office, he went through the speech in his head.

After about three minutes, a small man in a somewhat wrinkled suit came out. Colin stretched out to his full six-foot-two-inch frame. He was going to tower over this guy.

"Mr. Johnson." The guy had a firm handshake. A small man, but not a wimp. Colin swallowed down an instinctive smile.

"Mr. Steinberg, I own quite a bit of stock in SolarStar. But I've just found out you're in bed with some unsavory businesses. I'd like to talk in your office immediately."

CHAPTER 2

The email had come to him last week.

Someone called the Benefactor was hosting a contest. If Colin completed ten tasks ahead of the other three contestants, he'd win $10 million. There was a website, and it seemed legit. At least, as far as he could tell. And the Benefactor person or people seemed to know a *lot* about him. This was no email scam. This was personal.

> We, the Benefactor, wish you the best in securing money for your family's failing business. We also hope that your brother will be able to have the surgery he so desperately wants.

Danni's situation wasn't a secret. But no one besides Danni and their mom knew that their hardware store was on the verge of going bankrupt. Other than using the wrong pronoun for Danni, the Benefactor seemed to be an expert on the Burnett family. And it was true: a few million bucks wouldn't gather dust in Colin's household.

So he'd signed up.

For the first task, he had to go to a park in a rich part of Minneapolis and record a video of two people there: a pretty Latina girl about his age and a younger girl who looked like her sister. Then he'd uploaded the footage to the Contest's website. Easy enough.

The second task was weirder: He had to mail a snap cutter from his store to someone named Ana Rivera. She lived in the same super-fancy neighborhood where the park was, and Colin wondered if it was the same girl he had videotaped. He would bet his right arm that she was in this contest too. And that made him mad. How could she possibly need $10 million? She lived in mansion country.

Not that it mattered, because he was going to beat her.

As long as he got through this third task.

On the way to Mr. Steinberg's office, Colin made a point of looking from side to side, swiveling his body back and forth so the camera on his tie would catch as much as possible. Steinberg was walking in front of him and didn't seem to notice.

A woman stuck her head out of an office as they passed. "Len, I set up the meeting with Huffmann Industries for next Tues—"

"Thanks, Jennifer," said Steinberg, cutting her off. "I'll swing by later and touch base with you about that."

"OK. We only have one printout of the proposal. Should I just keep it in my file cabinet till—"

"That'll be fine, thanks."

The woman looked surprised, like she wasn't used to that sharp tone. But Steinberg had already moved on, with Colin trailing him.

Colin looked back over his shoulder. He twisted his torso as far around as he could so that the tie camera would catch the woman's puzzled face and the nameplate on her office door: Jennifer McKnight.

A moment later, he was sitting in Mr. Steinberg's office. But Steinberg looked as if he didn't want Colin to get too comfortable.

"So you're a shareholder, Mr. Johnson? You seem awfully young."

Colin tried not to shift uncomfortably in his seat. *Look natural. Act like you know what you're talking about.* "Yes. And I'm very upset about your new partnership." How was he going to get the bug under Steinberg's desk . . . ?

"What partnership?" demanded Steinberg.

Well, the Benefactor hadn't told Colin that. They'd only given him a list of vague complaints. The kind of stuff customers at the hardware store might say if they were trying to get a refund they didn't deserve. No specifics about the actual problem, just a lot of hot air.

Colin said, "You know which partnership." Then he got back on track with the speech: "If you think that your major investors are going to support this move, I assure you—"

"What move, Mr. Johnson? I'm still not sure we're on the same page." Steinberg didn't look like he was buying this.

Colin felt the sweat beading up on his lip. "Clearly not. If we were on the same page, you never would've betrayed your principles like this . . ."

Steinberg leaned forward in his chair. "Well, Mr. Johnson, I forgot to ask at the beginning here, but before I discuss any sensitive information with you, I should see your ID."

Crap. Could he get out of this somehow? "Is that really necessary, Mr. Steinberg?" Even if he did avoid showing his ID, Colin could tell Steinberg wasn't about to leave him alone in the office. He'd never have a chance to plant the bug . . .

"I'm afraid it is necessary," said Steinberg.

Colin knew his cover was blown. He stood up, almost knocking the chair over. "I don't think so, Mr. Steinberg. I will not be . . ." He backed up, toward the door. "I will not be . . . disrespected . . ."

And then he ran.

He didn't slow down until he got to the elevators, and then he speed-walked out of the building, expecting security guards to stop him at any moment. He could still feel the bug in his pocket, unplanted, mocking him.

He'd failed.

CHAPTER 3

Colin had a shift at the hardware store every weekday afternoon. This Monday was no different. Except that on most Mondays, Colin hadn't just skipped school and blown a chance to win $10 million.

He went around to the back of the building and unlocked the door that led to the family's apartment upstairs. Slowly, he climbed the narrow staircase and headed to his bedroom to change into more casual clothes. This yearbook-picture outfit wasn't exactly his typical work uniform.

His shift at the store started in five minutes.

His mom would be waiting for him to switch with her. And of course, she had no idea any of this was happening. He would need to act like everything was normal.

He flung his dad's tie onto the bed and sat down next to it. Ten million dollars, up in smoke. But it wasn't his fault. That task had been impossible. How was he supposed to *not* get caught when he didn't even know who he was dealing with or why he was there?

Would he hear anything from the Benefactor after this? An official "You're fired" message? Or would everything go to radio silence?

Colin pulled up his email account on his phone. And sure enough, a message from the Benefactor sat in his inbox.

Colin,

You have disappointed us greatly. You failed to plant the listening device at SolarStar. However, you did provide us with a fairly complete picture of the office's layout. Because of this, we will not disqualify you from the Contest. If you complete your fourth task as instructed,

you will receive a two-day suspension and
then continue to compete. For now, check
the website for your fourth task.

Colin practically fell down. He was still in
the Contest. He pulled up the website on his
phone and watched as the contestants' counters
came up.

He was still ahead. He was on Task 4, and
the other three contestants were on 3, 2, and 0.
He was good to go. The $10 million could still
be his. He couldn't believe his luck.

The top of the screen showed his new
instructions and time frame.

TASK 4

0:58

You still have the device that you failed to
plant at the SolarStar office. Deliver it to
the front door of Ana Rivera at 1200 Spring
Lake Parkway, Minneapolis, MN.

Ana Rivera—the same girl he'd sent the snap
cutter to. This was a super-easy task, especially
compared to the one he'd just failed. Colin knew

he should be relieved, and he was. But he was also puzzled. Why was he still in the Contest? The rules had been pretty clear: if you mess up a task, you're out.

But there wasn't time to wonder about it. He had only an hour to get to South Minneapolis. That meant he had to leave *now*.

Colin pulled the bug out of his pocket, grabbed a bubble envelope from his desk drawer, and stuffed the bug in. Then he dashed out into the narrow hallway and knocked on his sister's bedroom door. "Danni, are you in there?"

"Yeah, loser. What's up?"

"Can you cover the first half of my shift?" He felt bad asking. Danni had graduated high school last year, so she worked extra-long hours at the store now while she saved up for college— and for the operation. She didn't have much time to herself.

"Why? Where do you need to be?"

"I left a textbook at school, I have to go back for it. Tell Mom I'm sorry."

And then he was rocketing down the stairs,

knowing Danni wouldn't say no. Because either of them would do anything for the store—or for each other.

* * * * *

Ana's house was a mansion. It could literally hold ten buildings the size of his family's store/apartment. The house stood in the middle of a massive landscaped lawn. Colin had seen forest preserves with fewer plants than this lawn. And the car in the driveway had to be worth a fortune.

Most important: the mailbox was attached to the house, at the top of a huge flight of steps.

Colin's pace slowed as he got closer. The envelope with the bug in it crinkled in his clenched hand. During the bus ride down here, he'd written Ana's name on it—plus her address, just for good measure. But he knew it still wouldn't look legit: a random unstamped envelope showing up at four in the afternoon.

He just hoped he could do this without being seen. He'd just have to run up the stairs, stick the envelope in the mailbox, and run away. Not at all conspicuous, right?

He was halfway up the steps when the door started to open.

Crap.

Colin tossed the package onto the top step, spun around, and sprinted back down the steps. Then before the person stepped out, he dove behind the nearest manicured bush. It was a little sneakier than making a run for it out in the open.

He heard a disgusted noise from the doorway. "These *packages*!" A woman's voice. Definitely annoyed. Colin heard a brief crunching sound.

Then he heard the door slam and footsteps going down the stairs and over to the driveway. Colin hoped that if he still couldn't see her, that meant she also couldn't see him. But he didn't let out his breath until he heard the car start and then squeal away.

After another minute, he popped out from behind the bush and went back to his original plan: running like crazy.

He only paused long enough to notice that the bubble envelope was still lying on the top step. The woman hadn't moved it. In fact, it looked more crumpled than it had a minute ago. As if she'd stepped on it when she walked past.

Nice people, these Riveras, Colin thought as he ran.

When he got to the bus stop, he checked the website on his phone.

TASK 4 COMPLETE

Check back in twenty-four hours for your next task.

Success. Sort of.

A two-day suspension would give the other contestants time to catch up to him. But that just meant he'd have to work harder than ever. He could still pull this off. And the Benefactor clearly wanted him to stay in the running.

He frowned. *Why* had the Benefactor cut him a break?

As he waited for the bus, Colin thought over what he'd just done. He'd failed to plant a bug—and now it seemed like it was Ana's turn to try. Maybe *her* next task was to put that listening device under Len Steinberg's desk.

So that meant these tasks weren't random. The Benefactor actually wanted them all to be completed. For whatever reason.

If that was true, maybe the Benefactor didn't want *any* of the contestants to fail.

Which meant this wasn't actually a contest.

So what was it?

CHAPTER 4

"Hey, loser," Danni said as Colin walked up to the store's front counter. "Took you long enough."

"Shut up," Colin said, smiling. Then he added, "Thanks for covering for me."

"Sure thing." Danni was bent low over the counter, studying some printouts, her hair falling over her eyes.

"Everything go OK today?" Colin asked. He kept his voice casual, but of course Danni would know what he was asking. Did any of the customers give Danni crap? Sometimes people just started insulting her as soon as they saw her or heard her talk. Sometimes they threatened to take their business elsewhere if someone like her was working here. Sometimes it was just the looks— like Danni was a freak of nature or, worse, not natural at all. Colin had seen too many of those looks aimed at Danni when she was just trying to sell people their antifreeze and motor oil.

"Yeah, work's been fine." But she didn't look up from the printouts. Colin remembered how she hadn't opened her bedroom door when Colin talked to her earlier, asking her to take part of his shift. Danni didn't usually avoid eye contact unless she had a reason.

"Danni," Colin said, his voice stern.

"Yeah?"

"Look at me, will you?"

Danni sighed. Then raised her head. Sure enough, she had a black eye.

Colin's fists clenched at his sides. "Who did it?"

Danni shrugged. "Just ran into somebody from high school on the way to get groceries."

"Tell me who, Danni."

"Why? So you can go find them and get your ass kicked?"

"So I can go find them and teach them a lesson."

Danni walked out from behind the counter and put her hands on Colin's shoulders. "Little bro. That's not how it works. And it's not your job. People are going to be dumb. I knew that when I came out. It's just the way it is."

"But it shouldn't be! And what if you get really hurt? Trans people get *killed* sometimes . . ."

"I've told you, there's no point worrying about that. I can't live my life in fear."

But Colin couldn't help worrying.

Danni was transgender. And in some people's minds, that just wasn't allowed.

For the first thirteen years of Colin's life, he'd had an older brother—Daniel. They were just a year apart and had always been close. Then, three years ago, Daniel had come to Colin and their mom with some news. He'd never felt like a boy. He always felt like a girl— ever since he was little.

Apparently this was called *gender dysphoria*. Colin had to look it up. Since then, he'd learned all sorts of new terms and words. Cisgender, which was what Colin was—comfortable with the gender they were assigned at birth. And transgender—people who felt like their gender didn't match their biological sex. Colin also learned that gender wasn't just about being a boy or a girl. It had blown his mind.

His mom had cried a lot. But mostly because she was so sad about how hard things had been for Danni. And because she knew that a lot of people wouldn't understand that Danni really was a girl. A lot of people would find it scary. A lot of people would hate Danni. Mrs. Burnett didn't want Danni to have to go through that.

Colin's reaction hadn't been as cool as his mom's. He was only fourteen then, and he'd been embarrassed. Plus, this was older brother he had looked up to, turning out to be someone else. Colin felt betrayed.

But that turned into something different.

Respect. Admiration. Because Danni chose to be who she was no matter what anyone else said. That took more courage than Colin felt he had in his pinkie. Which was why he desperately wanted to get enough money for Danni to afford gender reassignment surgery, the operation that would make her a biological woman. Danni had dreamed of that operation for years. So that she could finally feel comfortable in her body. That was why Colin needed the Contest's prize money.

That, and . . .

Now that Danni had moved away from the paperwork, Colin got a good look at it. "Are these last month's numbers?"

Danni sighed. "Yep."

Everything in red. Like the month's before. And the month's before that.

In short, Burnett Hardware was in big trouble.

Like a tidal wave, the grief of losing his father washed over Colin again. It had been five years, and still the loss hit him like a ton of bricks, out of nowhere. His dad would have a scheme to make sure they got out of the red, or at least one that would make them laugh in the meantime. He was a risk-taker and an eternal optimist. Though Colin's mom was an optimist too, she was more down-to-earth. And she was sure they'd have to sell the store.

Both Danni and Colin hated that thought. It would be like losing their dad all over again.

Colin said, "Listen, we may not have to worry about it soon."

Danni furrowed her eyebrows. "Yeah, right. We're going to win the lottery?"

Colin shrugged and went behind the counter to stand in front of the computer. "Just . . . I may be working something out."

Danni looked at him intently. "Don't do anything crazy, brother, you understand? You're a little too much like Dad."

Colin grinned. "And that's a bad thing?"

Danni smiled back. "It's an awesome thing. And it's also scary. Dad had some great ideas, but he also got carried away sometimes. Unrealistic. And that made things worse."

Colin didn't like to think of his dad that way. But he knew Danni had a point. "Hey, don't worry about me," he said.

"Well, back at ya," said Danni as she headed toward the back of the store.

Easier said than done, thought Colin.

CHAPTER 5

All through his shift, Colin mulled over what Danni had said. The more he thought about it, the more the idea of prize money sounded far-fetched.

In fact it seemed much more likely that the Benefactor was just using him to do . . . something. Using all of the contestants. And once all the tasks were done, then what? The Benefactor had no reason to follow through and pay him. Colin had no way to hold him accountable. The whole thing—the website, the emails—could just be a giant scam.

Only instead of Colin giving away his bank

account or social security number, he'd given away his time, his effort. His *face*. The people at SolarStar would remember his face. If Ana planted that bug and then Steinberg found it— he'd remember the weird guy who pretended to be a shareholder. And if somebody used that snap cutter or that footage of the two girls— all that stuff could be traceable back to him. His fingerprints would be all over the snap cutter—same with the bug. And who would believe that some mysterious other person, or people, had told Colin to do these things? The police wouldn't buy it. Even if he showed them the website, the emails, all of that could be fake—something Colin himself had created. There might be a way to trace it back to the Benefactor . . . or there might not.

Colin paced behind the counter. This could be really bad. How had he not seen it before?

Upstairs in the apartment, he could hear his mom's voice and then Danni's. They were getting dinner ready, probably. He couldn't hear what they were saying, but their voices were calm, soothing.

Colin took a deep breath. He was getting carried away here. He didn't know what the Benefactor planned to do. He couldn't be *sure* that the prize money wasn't real.

But he could try to find out.

He had almost two days before his next task. That was plenty of time to figure out whether he wanted to stay in the Contest.

* * * * *

"So you decided to skip class this afternoon, huh?"

Colin's mom was waiting for him in the kitchen. His shift had just ended, and he'd switched off with Danni again. He'd been looking forward to supper—until now.

"Um. What?"

"The vice principal called. He said you were reported absent from your last class."

"Oh." He sat down at the table, trying to figure out what excuse he could give.

"Well?"

"Yeah. Sorry, Mom."

"That's it? What were you doing?"

"I . . . was hanging out with Drew and the guys."

His mom closed her eyes and put a hand to her forehead. "Were you drinking?"

"No!"

"Smoking?"

No, I was in downtown Minneapolis, trying to plant a bug in an office, because someone I don't know offered me a bunch of money. "Uh—maybe. Just a little."

"Is that why you were late to your shift? So I wouldn't smell it on you?"

"Mayyyybe."

And now for the lecture. Colin's mom didn't chew him out very often. Colin usually didn't give her any reason to. But when she did, she could really get going. Colin sat through it, looked sorry, promised not to do it again. But she still finished up with the clincher: "What do you think your father would say if he were here?"

Colin swallowed. "Probably that he expects better of me."

His mom sighed. "You're so bright, honey. And you work so hard. I just don't want you to do something you'll regret later."

"I know, Mom. It won't happen again."

But Colin was still thinking about his dad. If only he could ask his dad for advice—about all of this. Colin had no idea what his dad would think of the Contest.

But he knew what his mom would think. And Danni.

That it wasn't worth it. That it was dangerous and stupid, and that he needed to get out while he could.

"OK, honey," said his mom. She sounded exhausted. "I'm trusting you. Go ahead and eat before the food gets cold."

"Mom?"

"Yes?"

"You saw Danni's eye, right?"

Her jaw clenched. "I saw it. We talked. She says she's OK."

Colin stared at the fork in his hand. "I wish she didn't have to deal with this. I wish she could have the surgery . . ."

"That wouldn't change how some people see her, Colin. You know the surgery isn't a magic spell."

"No, but . . ." But if Danni could afford college. If she could move out of the family apartment, get a place of her own. If she didn't have to spend every spare minute working at the store. *And* if she had the surgery. All of these things together might add up to something closer to the life Danni deserved.

And none of it would be possible without some sort of magic spell.

Or ten million dollars.

He had to find out if it was real. He still hoped—for Danni's sake, for everyone's sake— that it could be.

CHAPTER 6

Alone in his room that night, Colin opened up his laptop. He needed to figure out what the Contest was really about—what all these tasks were building up to. Then he'd know whether the Benefactor could be trusted. Whether he'd really get the money if he won.

Colin started with what he knew: SolarStar. He had no trouble finding the company's website. They made environmentally friendly products—nothing super shady or exciting.

Next he looked up Huffmann Industries, the company Jennifer McKnight had mentioned. As soon as he clicked on their website, a flash player on the homepage played a video.

In the video, the sun came up over green grass, and then the pictures changed fast, like they were on fast-forward, to grass growing, clouds blowing, and then people walking. The pictures kept changing—smiling people of all different cultures in front of buildings or the ocean or mountains.

The voiceover said, "In a changing world, innovation is a precious commodity. And so are you. Here at Alfred Huffmann Industries, we provide what you need to keep up with the fast pace of a busy and fulfilling life."

There was more like that, all cheery and vague. When the video ended Colin sat back, frustrated. He'd learned nothing.

He clicked on a tab called "Companies." Apparently Huffmann Industries wasn't just one company. It was almost a dozen—all owned by the same person or people, Colin guessed. These companies did a lot of manufacturing, but other than that they didn't seem to have much in common. There were also companies that looked like charities—the Huffmann

Cancer Foundation and an international medical group called Doctors Together. But SolarStar wasn't listed anywhere. Probably because Huffmann Industries didn't own SolarStar, Colin figured. Maybe the two companies were just working together on a one-time project. And maybe that project hadn't started yet? Or maybe it was top secret?

Either way, this was probably the partnership the Benefactor had told Colin to complain about.

So maybe the Benefactor was unhappy about Huffmann Industries and SolarStar working together. Maybe the Benefactor was an investor in SolarStar, a real-life version of the fake Ray Johnson whom Colin had pretended to be. After all, SolarStar was focused on the environment, and Huffmann Industries wasn't, as far as Colin could tell. In fact, Colin was pretty sure manufacturing tended to involve pollution and damage to natural resources. At least that's what Danni had said when she was taking that class about climate.

All right: maybe someone connected with

SolarStar was angry about SolarStar teaming up with Huffmann Industries. He was making a lot of guesses here, but if he could find that person, he might just find the Benefactor.

So now he had to think of a way to do that. Colin looked at the ceiling for inspiration. He couldn't just find a list of the company's shareholders online. Hundreds of people could own stock in SolarStar. Maybe thousands— though it seemed like small company, so Colin doubted it had a ton of investors. Still—the Benefactor could be anyone.

He typed "Huffmann Industries SolarStar partnership" into the search bar. No helpful hits. All he found were several articles about a possible deal between Huffmann Industries and an oil company called ChemOil. The most recent article was about six months old, and it said that the deal had fallen through.

Colin started to scroll more, but something about the article pinged with him. One minute Huffmann Industries was ready to work with an oil company, and then next minute they were getting cozy with a green energy company? Oil and green energy were as close to opposites as you could get. You might as well buy a fitness center and a candy store at the same time.

Except that the deal with ChemOil hadn't actually happened. And the deal with SolarStar either *had* happened or was about to happen. Colin wondered if anyone involved with ChemOil knew about that. Probably not, if the partnership was still secret or not final yet. But people at Huffmann Industries—they'd know what was going on. And some of them might not like it.

So someone at SolarStar could be mad the company was partnering with Huffmann Industries. Or someone at Huffmann Industries was mad they were partnering with SolarStar and not ChemOil.

In short: it could still be anyone.

Colin skimmed back through the most recent article about the deal falling through with ChemOil, looking for more clues. It quoted Corinne Huffmann, the CEO of Huffmann Industries. "The environmental cost of their proposed pipeline would've outweighed its many benefits. Though I'm disappointed in this outcome, we are committed to working toward sustainable energy solutions. That's good for the planet, and it's good business."

Meanwhile, an anonymous source—a Huffmann Industries "insider"—had said something very different. "Walking away from this deal was a mistake, whether Corinne will admit it or not. ChemOil's business leadership is unmatched. You can't replace that with a bunch of half-baked ideas about 'environmental friendliness.' That doesn't amount to anything more than a bunch of sunshine and rainbows. It certainly doesn't amount to dollar signs."

Whoa, though Colin, *that's harsh*. Whoever this person was, he or she sounded pissed.

Pissed enough to want to mess up Huffmann Industries' new deal with SolarStar? Pissed enough to design a complicated contest just to make that happen? If that was the case, the Benefactor wasn't connected to SolarStar. He or she was connected to Huffmann Industries.

And, of course, he or she was still nameless. So far.

Colin lay in bed, and for the first time in a long time, felt his mind calm down enough to feel sleepy. Ever since the contest had started, sleep had become its own dream. But finally, he was getting somewhere. With a small smile, he shut his eyes and drifted off immediately.

CHAPTER 7

Wednesday afternoon, after school, Colin kept checking his watch. He only had one more hour till his suspension ended and he could get back into the Contest—if he wanted to. He still couldn't decide. He hadn't been able to find any more information since Monday night. His researching was just turning up dead ends and vague business-y stuff he didn't understand.

An Asian girl around his age walked into the store.

Colin put on a smile and said, "Hey there. Can I help you?"

The girl started like she'd been kicked. "Uh,

no. I'm just looking for . . . a hammer." Colin saw her neck working as she swallowed.

"Second aisle from the back, about halfway down."

"Thanks." She gave him a deer-in-the-headlights look as she walked past. He narrowed his eyes. Lots of people liked to steal things from the store. Maybe he should walk with her . . .

Just then, the phone rang behind the register. The rule was: always answer the phone. Plus, he could see the people in the mirror on the ceiling, which was supposed to help catch shoplifters. He'd keep an eye on the girl.

He wouldn't mind doing that either. She was pretty cute, in a serious, buttoned-up kind of way.

He called, "Let me know if you need anything else," and picked up the phone, angling his body so that he could watch the mirror.

"Hello?"

Silence. He couldn't even hear breathing on the other end. "Hello?" he said, this time a little angry. He didn't have time for this.

"Listen, I'm going to hang up. But thanks for wasting my time."

"You've been busy." The voice was a man's—deep, a little unsteady. "The Benefactor does not approve. Your curiosity could cause problems for you."

Colin's palms were slick with sweat. He could barely hold onto the phone. "Who is this?"

"Do not question the Benefactor. You will be told all you need to know." The voice on the other end was definitely wobbling. With nervousness? It also sounded as if he was reading off a script. But that didn't make it any less terrifying for Colin. "It would be dangerous for you to know more than the Benefactor tells you. Very. Dangerous."

"*Who are you?*" Colin hissed.

Then all he heard was the dial tone. He stared at the phone stupidly. When the store's front door clanged shut, he jumped. He realized the girl had left and he hadn't been checking the mirror to see what she was doing.

He turned back to the register and saw something that hadn't been there before. A hammer sat on the counter. Beneath it was a note:

Do not displease us again. Or it will be the last nail in your coffin.

CHAPTER 8

Colin couldn't stop shaking. The phone call, the threat . . . *a death threat*. Every doubt he'd had about this Contest exploded into real fear. The stakes had suddenly gotten very, very high.

The Benefactor knew he'd been doing research. How?

Bugs. Of course. There could be a camera somewhere in the apartment. Or a keystroke tracker on his computer. Or . . .

But that was ridiculous. How would anyone get into his apartment to plant bugs?

He stared down at the note. It didn't matter *how*. The Benefactor knew what he was up to. Had been watching him. And now Colin had been warned. He wasn't supposed to ask questions or do research or try to figure out what was really going on.

Colin crumpled up the note. Part of him wanted to email the Benefactor and say he was quitting. But part of him thought that the best way to find out more was to keep playing along. Do some more tasks. Maybe some pieces would start to fit together and make sense.

He kept remembering the girl's face. He recognized the look she'd given him. Terror. Doing something she didn't really want to do. She had to be a contestant. And he was pretty sure she wasn't Ana Rivera. That meant he knew three of the four people in the Contest: Ana, this girl, and himself. Maybe he wasn't the only one in the dark here. Or maybe he was. Either way, if he could talk to one of the other contestants, he might get more information.

As long as he could do it without the Benefactor knowing.

The alarm on his watch went off. His suspension from the Contest was over.

Colin turned to the computer at the counter and pulled up a web browser.

TASK 5

Go to Olsen High School tonight after sundown. Wait for a boy on a bicycle to arrive. Take the bicycle without being seen and bring it home.

Colin huffed out a breath. Seriously? Stealing a bike? This told him nothing about the Benefactor's master plan.

At least this task was in his own neighborhood. At his own high school, in fact. It would be convenient, if nothing else. And maybe he'd learn something he wasn't expecting. Maybe the boy on the bike was also involved in the Contest. If so, Colin could try to talk to him—find out if this dude knew more than he did.

He would just need an excuse to leave the apartment tonight without making his mom suspicious. Right now, that seemed like the least of his worries.

* * * * *

"Hey, Mom, I'm going over to Matt's to study for our history test."

His mother eyed him carefully. "Is Matt going to be the only one there?"

"What? Yeah."

"So not Drew and whoever else you were with when you skipped class on Monday?"

"Oh. That."

"Yes, Colin. That. I'm not crazy about the idea of you getting high with your friends on a weeknight. Or any night."

"We'll just be studying, Mom. And it'll just be Matt and me."

"So if I were to call Matt right now, he'd say the same thing?'

"Yeah." He kept his face as innocent as possible, hoping his mom wouldn't call his bluff.

She smiled. A tired smile. "All right then, honey. I'm trusting you." Colin's stomach clenched. This was maybe the worst part about the whole thing. Lying to his mom. Especially because she *did* trust him. "Now I gotta get back to the store." She kissed him on the cheek, and Colin swallowed down his conscience.

* * * * *

Fall in Minneapolis was just plain cold. Colin shivered in the bushes across the street from his high school. He adjusted his body so that his shins were the only thing in contact with the ground. It was 1:30. He'd been out here for hours, way longer than he'd expected. His mom was going to be completely pissed when he finally got back.

But the guy with the bike still hadn't showed up. Colin felt he had no choice but to keep waiting.

From the corner of his eye, he saw movement. An African American guy about his age rode up on a bike. That must be *the* bike. And this must be the last contestant.

The kid rode right up to the bushes where Colin was crouched. Colin ducked down farther. He wanted to talk to this guy, but first he needed to make sure he wasn't walking into trouble.

He heard the kid rummaging around in some kind of bag. Then the clink of cans. The clinking continued, fainter and fainter, as the guy crossed the street.

Colin peeked over the top of the bush.

The bike was resting right in front of him. Its owner was standing in front of the school now. The guy looked around—left, right, left again. *Nervous*, thought Colin. Then the guy started to spray paint the wall.

Well, this kid didn't seem that threatening. Colin figured he could approach him without putting himself in danger.

He straightened up and opened his mouth to call out to the guy—then froze.

Spray-painted red letters had taken shape on the wall of his school: *CB*

Colin's initials. His stomach clenched. The guy kept spray painting, working fast.

we know

This was a message. A message for him. And it had to be from the Benefactor. This guy was definitely part of the Contest.

about your brother.

Danni. This person was threatening Danni. Calling her "your brother." Could this spray painter be the same person who had beaten Danni up the other day?

time is running out

Colin felt numb. The threats this afternoon had been bad enough. But this—this crossed a line.

He had to get out of here. He had to make sure Danni was safe.

Without thinking, Colin grabbed the bike and got on. He shouldered the guy's backpack, which had been resting on the handlebars. And then he took off, pedaling as fast as he could.

As he pedaled, the rage and fear faded just enough to let him think. The Benefactor wasn't just using the contestants to do big tasks. He was using them against each other. *Contestant Three, leave a threatening note for Colin. Contestant Four, spray paint a threat on Colin's high school wall. Colin, steal Contestant Four's bike.*

There was no doubt in Colin's mind now. This Contest was a trap. And the Benefactor wasn't just shady or mysterious.

This person was evil.

CHAPTER 3

The guy's backpack was empty, so Colin couldn't learn anything from that. He stashed it with the bike behind the dumpster in the tiny parking lot behind the store. Someone could come along and steal it again by morning, but Colin had bigger problems to deal with.

"WHERE HAVE YOU BEEN?"

As soon as Colin walked into the apartment, his mom practically tackled him. She looked scared—really scared. As scared as he felt. Which was weird, because she wasn't the one caught up in the Contest.

"I'm sorry, Mom, I really am—"

"I called Matt's, he said you weren't there. I called your phone, you didn't answer."

"I—"

"What is going on, Colin? Just tell me!"

She looked like she'd been crying. A lot. Colin had a sinking feeling in his chest. His mom never cried in front of them. She might get mad, she might worry, but not like this. He hadn't seen her this close to a total breakdown since his dad died.

"Are you OK, Mom? Is everybody OK?" If something had happened to Danni . . .

"No, I'm not OK! You disappeared! It's almost two in the morning, and I couldn't get hold of you—"

Danni came running out of her room. She looked at Colin and sighed with relief. But then gave him the stink eye as she turned toward their mom. "Mom, don't do this right now. Let's all just get some sleep and talk things through in the morning."

To Colin's relief, Danni looked fine. Other than the black eye, which was fading. And the glare she was giving Colin. "Go back to bed, Mom. We'll deal with it in the morning."

Danni managed to coax Mrs. Burnett back to bed, but when Colin started to go to his own room, Danni grabbed his arm.

"Mom's freaked out because she found a threatening note at the store. She thinks it was for me."

The note. Hadn't he thrown it away? He remembered crumpling it up. But he must've left it on the counter. The words were burned into his brain: *Do not displease us again. Or it will be the last nail in your coffin.* Vague enough to mean just about anything.

Danni was looking hard at Colin. "So. Are you going to tell me what you're doing?" She sounded eerily like their mother.

"I—it's a long story."

The look on Danni's face was one Colin had never seen there before. Disappointment, mixed with something like anger mixed with something like fear. "Well, you'd better come up with something better than *that* by tomorrow morning."

* * * * *

Colin got maybe two hours of sleep. Maybe. In the morning he told his mom he'd lied to her. Which was true. Just not for the reasons she thought.

"Look, Mom, the thing is—I kind of have a girlfriend."

His mom and sister stared at him across the kitchen table. For a minute Colin thought they didn't buy it.

Then Danni broke into a grin. "Are you serious? Why didn't you just say so?"

Colin shrugged. "I dunno. It wasn't, like, official till last night. Didn't want to jinx it, I guess."

"Who is it?" Danni demanded.

"Nobody you know."

"I'm not surprised. I don't know anyone in their right mind who'd date you."

Colin smiled in spite of himself. "I didn't say she was in her right mind."

Danni laughed. "What's her name, at least?"

Before Colin had to make up a name, his mom cut in. "You could have at least texted me last night to let me know you were safe."

"I know. I'm really sorry. I—we fell asleep."

"Too much information," said Danni.

"Hey, you asked."

Their mom let out a long breath. "Well, I have to admit I'm relieved. I was afraid—I don't know. I didn't know what to think. But you shouldn't have disappeared. There's no excuse for that."

"You're right," Colin said, and he meant it.

He'd dodged one bullet, at least. Danni was back to teasing him. Their mom was back to looking only generally worried instead of panicked to death.

But Colin knew the Benefactor was still watching him. Trying to control him. And willing to hurt his family if he didn't do as he was told.

* * * * *

The guy's bike was still out back where he'd left it. Colin figured he might as well ride it to school and lock it up there till he figured out what to do with it. When he lifted up the backpack, he realized it wasn't empty anymore. A small envelope peeked out from the partly unzipped front pocket. It couldn't have been there long, or it would've been stolen by now.

Right on cue, Colin's hands started sweating. Was this another threat?

He tore open the envelope and pulled out a credit card. With his name on it.

And there was another card in there too. A driver's license. It looked exactly the same as Colin's license. Except that it said he was twenty-five years old.

This couldn't possibly be as awesome as it looked.

Then he took out the last item in the envelope: a typed note.

Colin: Check the website for your next task. Only use the credit card and ID as instructed.

Yeah. This couldn't be good.

When he put the note back into the envelope, though, he noticed some tiny handwriting on the inside of the envelope. He squinted to see what it said.

Meet me at tonight at 8:00 p.m. in the Minneapolis Central Library. 1st floor, Nonfiction, Me-Na. Signed, Hammer Girl.

CHAPTER 10

The graffiti seemed to take up the entire west wall of Olsen High School. Colin tried not to look at it as he rode up and locked the stolen bike at a bike rack. *Don't think about the threats. Think about how to stop this.*

Before he could decide whether to meet the mysterious girl, Colin had to check the Contest's website. He brought it up on his phone.

TASK 6

Go to the tobacco shop on Lowry Avenue by 5:00 p.m. Ask for Pablo and tell him you would like to buy some venison. He will provide you with a gun, ammunition, and a

diagram of the gun's parts. Use the credit
card to pay him. Then take the gun apart
and put it in a bubble envelope with the
bullets and the diagram. Deliver the package
to Ana Rivera by 10:00 p.m. Saturday.

So he had to buy a gun. Colin was *not*
prepared for that.

He found himself pacing, wiping his hands
off on his jeans, his mind racing.

Then he stopped. Of course. He knew what
to do. The simplest solution.

He could quit.

He could end all of this right now, at least
for himself and his family.

Colin pulled up his email account and sent
the Benefactor a message. *I'm out. I withdraw
from the Contest.*

There. That felt better.

* * * * *

The second Colin walked into the store, he
knew something was wrong. His mom looked
completely spooked.

"Mom? What's going on?"

"Well, for one thing, someone smashed our back window this afternoon. Did you see?"

"I missed it." The Benefactor again?

"And for another thing, I think someone stole our insurance papers for the store."

"*What*? Why would someone do that?"

"I don't know, honey. But that's not what shook me up most. When I called the insurance company to let them know and ask for replacement papers, they said we didn't exist. We aren't in their database. Which means we have to start from scratch with a new policy. With money we don't have. And until we can get the new policy . . . well. We have to cover any damages to the store ourselves."

Colin swore and slammed his fist on the countertop. His mom jumped. "Sorry, Mom," he mumbled. "This is just—awful."

And he was 100 percent sure it was his fault.

"It probably won't end up being a problem," his mom said. He could tell she was trying to keep it together, for his sake. "It just rattled me a little. But don't worry about it. Let me just run this report, and then the store's all yours."

While his mom ran a sales report on the computer, Colin pulled out his phone and checked his email. Sure enough, Benefactor had responded to his message.

> We regret to inform you that withdrawal from the Contest is impossible. If you want to protect your family and their business, you will continue to compete.

So the Benefactor wouldn't let him quit. And if Colin insisted on backing out—refused to do the next task—something terrible might happen to his family.

He had to buy that gun.

"Uh, Mom, I gotta go, really sorry, back in forty-five minutes!"

And he was out the door before she could call after him.

* * * * *

At the dirty little tobacco shop, Pablo handed Colin a pistol, some ammunition, and a piece of paper. The guy smiled in a creepy way when he saw Colin's sweaty, shaky hands.

Colin was too freaked out to be offended. He just stuffed everything into his backpack, turned on his heel, and practically ran out of the shop.

He didn't even want to guess what the gun might be for. But it made the Benefactor's threats seem even more real. The stakes were getting painfully high.

If he didn't have to get back to the hardware store, he would take the gun to Ana's house right away. He didn't want this thing anywhere near him. But as it was, he'd probably have to wait to deliver it until Saturday.

Meanwhile, he'd meet Hammer Girl tonight.

Colin was pretty sure the Benefactor didn't know about Hammer Girl's note. And even if Colin's home was bugged, it didn't seem likely that the Benefactor had also planted cameras or listening devices in the downtown public library. It wasn't like Colin spent a lot of time hanging out there. So if he played this right, the Benefactor wouldn't know Colin was meeting with Hammer Girl. And maybe Hammer Girl wanted to find a way out of this mess too. If they could work together, behind the Benefactor's back, they might come up with a plan. A plan that involved everyone getting out of this Contest alive.

CHAPTER 11

When Colin got back to the store, his mom was almost too worn out to give him a hard time. Almost. He let her think he'd dashed off to see his new girlfriend. To make up for it, he promised to finish up the shift at the shop and then do inventory for the next three days. That was enough to quiet his mom down. But not enough to make her feel any better. Colin could see how disappointed she was and how confused. He'd never done anything like this before. Even if it was all because of a girl, it didn't make sense. He was worrying her.

But she'd be even more worried if she knew the truth.

At seven, Danni came in to take over at the register.

"Hey loser, go get supper. Mom made really good stew."

Colin could smell the gravy and vegetables wafting off of Danni. His stomach grumbled.

Colin shouldered his backpack. "Um, I can't, actually. I have plans."

Danni frowned. "What plans? Not the girlfriend *again*. Mom said you skipped half your shift to hang out with her earlier."

Colin shrugged, trying to act casual. "Well, I like her a lot. And she likes me."

"Colin, you're going to give Mom a heart attack if you keep this up. Can't you just stop being so secretive about it? You're acting really shifty. It's weirding us out."

"Yeah, well, it's about time I was the weird one, don't you think?" He regretted the words as soon as they were out of his mouth. They sounded awful—cruel. Danni looked as if he'd punched her in the stomach. "I didn't mean it like that—"

"How *did* you mean it?"

"I just—"

"Don't bother. I don't need to hear more lies. Go ahead—go see whoever it is you're seeing." The hurt showed in her eyes.

"Danni."

"I told you, I don't want to hear it." She didn't believe him. She didn't believe the girlfriend was real. Colin could read it in her face. She thought Colin was doing something shady. And she was right.

Colin didn't know what else to say, so he left.

* * * * *

Colin cursed his palms. Why did he have such an obvious tell when he was nervous? Why couldn't his reaction to nerves be a cool, strong presence? He wiped sweat off his upper lip. The library felt insanely hot.

At 8:02, according to his watch, Hammer Girl peeked around a bookshelf. Colin waved and then felt like an idiot. She'd left him a threatening note. Should you wave at someone who does that? For all he knew, she was working for the Benefactor by choice, and this was some kind of trap.

She came over to stand next to him, looking at the books on the shelf. "Do you know the Benefactor?" she whispered.

Colin swallowed and pretended to look at books, too. "Yes."

"There's a study room in the back. Let's go there to talk. I'll go first. Then you follow in five minutes. The Benefactor probably can't bug a place like this, but they could still have spies watching us. So it's better to be safe than sorry."

And with that, she disappeared.

The next five minutes were the longest in Colin's life. Finally, he sneaked to the back room and opened the door.

The girl sat at the table in the tiny, windowless room.

"Come on in, Colin. We have a lot to talk about."

CHAPTER 12

Colin sat down across from her and looked her in the eyes. Really pretty, serious brown eyes.

"Who are you?" he asked.

She looked at him steadily. "My name is Maiv Moua. I'm working for the Benefactor—just like you, and Ana Rivera, and James Trudeleau."

James Trudeleau must be the spray painter.

"You seem to know a lot about the situation," he said, trying to keep his voice neutral.

Maiv's eyes flashed. "I'm finding out as much as I can. But the Benefactor is a bit . . . shy."

Colin let out a surprised chuckle before he

could stop himself. "Yeah, that's one way of phrasing it."

"And meanwhile, they're putting us at risk. And our families."

Colin nodded. Could he trust her? He hoped so. It didn't seem too likely that she was the only contestant who *wasn't* an unwilling pawn in this game.

Still, he shouldn't let his guard down just yet. He leaned forward. "Why did you agree to do this contest?"

Maiv seemed to think for a second, tucking her hair behind her ears. Colin tried really hard to stop noticing how pretty she was. But he couldn't help it.

She took a deep breath. "I have six younger brothers and sisters. My mother has three jobs, and my dad can't work because of a back injury, and we have hardly any health insurance. I could get a full ride to just about anywhere for college—except I can't leave my family right now. My mom can barely manage as it is. If we had money, my dad could get the help he needs, and my mom wouldn't have to work herself to death. And I could go to college. That was the dream, anyway."

Colin nodded. And he made a decision: he would believe her. "Yeah. I get it. I need the money to keep my family's store running and—"

"I'm pretty sure we all need it," Maiv cut in. "That's why the Benefactor approached us. But the Benefactor isn't interested in helping us."

"Right," said Colin. "They're interested in using us to do their dirty work, and then framing us for whatever it is. And it's scaring the crap out of me at this point. They've threatened my family, and my latest task was to buy a gun. I'm supposed to deliver it to Ana by Saturday night."

Maiv nodded. She didn't look shocked to hear that a gun was in the mix. "We need to put an end to this before someone gets hurt."

"I'm with you there," said Colin. "I was hoping it would help to figure out what the endgame is. Why they're doing all this. It has to be part of a master plan."

"I think so too. I just haven't been able to figure out what that plan is."

"Well, one of my tasks was to go to SolarStar, and someone there mentioned Huffman Industries. So I've been looking into that . . ."

Maiv's face went blank with confusion. "SolarStar? Huffmann Industries? I haven't heard of either of these places."

"They're businesses. I think they're working together on some kind of top secret project, and someone wants that project to fail. Someone connected to Huffmann Industries, I'm guessing." He quickly outlined what he'd learned from his research. Maiv listened intently. By the time he finished, she looked impressed.

"This is great, Colin. Now that I know these businesses are involved, I can hack into their systems and—"

"Whoa, you can *what*?"

"Oh. Yeah." Maiv blushed. "I—I can hack into almost anything. It's—just a hobby. I just like knowing how things work, being able to find my way around a firewall. The challenge of it, you know. I don't ever do anything destructive, like steal information or . . ." Her voice trailed off, and she suddenly looked guilty.

"Well, I think that's an awesome skill," said Colin. "At least if you're using it to snoop on the Benefactor and not on me." He grinned, though he felt a little embarrassed to be joking at a time like this.

Maiv didn't smile back. In fact, she looked more upset than ever. "Colin, I *did* use it on you. I hacked into your insurance company's database and erased the records of your family's insurance."

Colin felt the grin drain off his face. So that's what had happened. That's why the insurance company had no record of the Burnett policy.

"It was a task," Maiv added quickly. "The Benefactor told me to do it. I—I felt awful about it. And I didn't realize then that your store was—failing."

"It's not your fault," said Colin. "And my mom is getting us a new policy, so I'm sure it'll be fine. Not that it won't be expensive." He tried to slip back into a cheerful tone. "Another reason I really could've used that prize money!"

This time, Maiv managed a small smile. "I'll settle for getting to the bottom of this."

"Deal."

"So listen. We should probably split up now. We've been out of the Benefactor's sight for too long, and I don't want them to get suspicious. But I've got an email address the Benefactor doesn't know about. I wrote it down in here."

She took a tiny notebook out of her pocket. It looked like an old-fashioned reporter's notebook. Colin flipped it open and saw the email address written on the first page. He was about to tear out the page, but Maiv said, "Just keep the whole notebook. I have a million of them."

"Old-school," said Colin. "Not what I'd expect of a hacker. You're just full of surprises."

Maiv flashed another smile, her first real one. "Comes in handy when some creep is digitally stalking you."

Colin tried to clear his head. Now was not the time to flirt.

Except . . . maybe she was flirting back? Just a little?

"You should create a new email account for yourself too," Maiv added. Back to business. "Make sure you don't do anything on your home computers, or your phone, or some other device the Benefactor could monitor. Use a public computer. And then let me know when you find out more, and I'll do the same."

Colin nodded, trying to take it all in. "I'll make a new email tonight before I go home. I'll use one of the computers here, at the library. And I'll send you a message so you'll have my new contact info."

"Sounds good." Maiv stood up to leave, then paused and put her hand on his arm. "We're going to get through this. Trust me."

CHAPTER 13

Danni wouldn't talk to Colin the next day. Colin tried to apologize for what he'd said, but he just got the silent treatment. He didn't have much more luck with his mom. They both knew he was hiding something from them. And until he came clean about whatever it was—or until he started acting normal again—they weren't interested in more excuses.

He put off delivering the gun as long as he could. But on Saturday night he dropped it off at the house. He made sure to be back by ten and in bed by ten-thirty so that his mom wouldn't have one more reason not to trust him. His seventh task, whatever it was, could wait until tomorrow. He fell asleep with his clothes on, too worn out to even bother undressing.

Less than two hours later, he woke with a bang. A literal bang.

At first he thought it was a gunshot. He rolled off his bed and onto the floor.

But after a second, he recognized the high whistling and cracks. Fireworks, not shots.

Colin heard his mom out in the hallway. "Are you guys OK?"

"Yeah," he called back, heading to his door.

Across the hall, Danni opened her door too. The three of them stood there in the hall staring at each other.

"Well," said Danni dryly. "That was quite a way to wake up."

But then Colin smelled it. Smoke. "Wait a minute . . ." He ran back into his room and looked out the window. Smoke curled under the sill.

He heard Danni swear and his mom cry out. Half a second later, all three of them were running downstairs. They burst outside just in time to see the wooden wall and roof overhang catch fire.

Colin's mom pulled out her phone to dial 9-1-1.

"Water," said Colin. "We need water." He started toward the apartment door, thinking he'd fill a bucket at the kitchen sink.

Danni grabbed him and pulled him back. "Don't go back in there, idiot!"

"We need water!"

"Then let's find someone with a hose! Don't go into a burning building, for the love of . . ."

Colin saw people gathering on the sidewalk. He spotted a neighbor with her robe on. "Water!" He screamed. "Does anyone have water?" But most of his neighbors just stood there. Colin could do nothing but watch as his family's business, their livelihood, and his dad's legacy burned.

Finally, Colin heard the fire trucks. The red and blue lights swirled around him. He felt dizzy, watching everything as if he was outside of his body. The firefighters found a hydrant and began spraying the building, now almost totally engulfed in flames. Colin felt water on his face but realized it was from tears. And then the three of them—Colin, Danni, and their mom—were hugging harder than he had ever hugged anybody in his whole life.

When the police showed up, Mrs. Burnett talked to them, while Colin broke away from the huddle and paced.

Their insurance papers were gone. Any record of their insurance policy had been erased. The business couldn't recover from something like this. And it couldn't be an accident. The Benefactor must've arranged it.

He kept pacing, swallowing back more tears. What kind of sick message was the Benefactor sending him now? Did they know Colin had met with Maiv? Or were they just trying to raise the stakes even more—make Colin even more desperate to win that prize money? Did the Benefactor really think he was stupid enough to still think the money was real?

Colin was so angry that it took him several seconds to notice a pair of eyes in the parking lot, peeking out from behind his mom's car. He knew that face. He knew her.

Ana.

Danni and Mrs. Burnett were still talking to the police. No one was looking at him or at the girl. Colin walked toward the car.

Ana flinched. He saw tears on her face. She put her finger to her lips. "He may be watching," she whispered. Colin nodded. He turned away from her to look back at the fire.

"I'm so sorry. This fire is my fault. I didn't realize . . ."

Colin shook his head and clenched his fists. It *wasn't* Ana's fault. They were all pawns in this terrible game.

Through the rage, he choked out the only words that mattered. "We have to find the Benefactor."

CHAPTER 14

Colin and Ana exchanged their secret email addresses and promised to be in touch. Colin also warned Ana that there was a gun waiting for her at her house. Then Ana sneaked away while the firefighters were still putting out the blaze.

By the time the police and firefighters left, the Burnetts were too weary to talk. The store was wrecked—most of their inventory was ruined or at least slightly damaged. Luckily, the building hadn't been completely destroyed. The apartment was smoky but mostly intact. Still, they couldn't stay there tonight.

The three of them piled into the family car, found the cheapest motel in the area, and grabbed a room. Despite feeling completely wired, Colin fell asleep almost instantly.

When he woke up, his first thought was *I need to get to a public computer*. But it was Sunday morning, so only a few libraries would only be open, and not till later in the day. So instead he checked the Contest website.

TASK 7

6:00

Go to Budget Car Rental on Hiawatha Avenue in South Minneapolis and pick up a van. The reservation has been made already. Use the ID and credit card given to you. Park the van near your motel and leave it there until further instructions.

Great. A van. His next task was probably to kidnap someone or move a body. This had gotten completely out of control.

Well, at least by the time he got the van and parked back here, a few of the public libraries would be open. Then he could get in touch with Maiv and Ana.

Danni and Mrs. Burnett were still asleep when Colin slipped out of the room.

* * * * *

At a library computer, Colin logged on to his new, secret email account. Almost immediately, a chat window popped up. It was Maiv, sending him an instant message.

Colin, are you there?

Colin quickly typed back: *Yeah.* Should he mention what had happened to the store? No, better start with business. *I just got Task 7. It was to pick up a van. A sketchy white van. I'm pretty creeped out.*

Well, that makes sense, came her response.

Colin typed, *How so?*

It took a while for her next message to come through. *I just got my ninth task. It's to run away tonight. I'm supposed to leave a note for my parents telling them not to look for me. I suspect all four of us will get the same task. The Benefactor is setting things up to look as if we're runaways. That way no* one will be surprised when we turn up missing.

What? Colin typed as fast as he could: *Turn up missing? What do you mean?*

Colin—I think the Benefactor is going to have us killed.

CHAPTER 15

Colin couldn't think for a minute. His mind was completely blank. Finally he typed back, *That's insane. They'd never get away with killing us!*

Why not? Maiv responded. *No one else knows about the Benefactor. He's scared all of us into not telling anyone. And if our families find notes in our own handwriting, saying we're running away, what other conclusion could they draw? Four kids who have nothing to do with each other—no obvious connection—except that they happen to be runaways. What does that say to you?*

Colin typed frantically, not caring if he made a million typos. *But they'd check on our emails and see that we were connected by this*

Benefactor dude and the Contest website.

Maiv didn't hesitate: *Don't you think the Benefactor has ways to wipe the emails? They've bugged our homes, our phones, everything. And they know at least as much about hacking as I do. I'm pretty sure they'll have no trouble erasing any evidence that the Contest ever existed.*

Colin thought for a long moment. Finally he typed, *Then we need to go to the police. Now.*

Her response was lightning-fast. *No way. Do you really think the police would believe two high school kids about something like this? Not without proof. And I mean real proof: proof of who the Benefactor is.*

Colin nodded slowly, even though he knew Maiv couldn't see him. *Fair enough,* he typed. *So for now we keep playing along?*

Yes. I hate to hurt my parents, but we can't risk making the Benefactor angry until we have enough info to expose him.

Colin's palms were practically dripping with sweat. *This is crazy,* he typed.

Maiv typed back, *Yep. Keep me posted.*

She logged off. Next Colin checked the Contest's website.

TASK 7 COMPLETE

Follow the next steps to win the Contest.

So this was it. Colin took a deep breath.

TASK 8

Write your family a handwritten note saying that you are running away. Tell them you do not want to cause them any more financial burden. Leave the motel by 11 p.m. tonight. Bring the envelope you've received with you. When you leave, the first half of your prize money—$5 million—will be given to your family.

Colin paused. Envelope? What envelope?

And then he saw it. Sitting on the corner of his computer table, inches from his right hand. It hadn't been there a minute ago. It was labeled *JAMES*.

Colin looked around. The library wasn't super crowded, but he saw no trace of Ana, James, or Maiv. So who had just put that envelope next to him?

The Benefactor? Or someone else who worked for the Benefactor—someone besides the four contestants?

Stay calm, he told himself. Unless someone had been looking directly over his shoulder for the past five minutes, no spy could've known that he was messaging Maiv. And simply using a library computer shouldn't make the Benefactor suspicious. After all, the Burnett home was a smoky mess, Colin hadn't taken his laptop with him, and the motel was a dump. Those were all good, innocent reasons for him to be here. Anyway, whoever had left the envelope had clearly been working fast, not hanging around to see what he was up to.

Colin suppressed a shudder and went back to reading.

TASK 9

Park the van at the corner of Nicollet Mall and Jefferson Avenue. Look for an African American boy in front of the SolarStar building. Slip the envelope into his pocket without speaking to him. Then return to the van.

TASK 10

Three other people will join you in the van. Drive to West River Parkway and wait by the

park across from the river. There, you will
receive $5 million, the second half of your
prize money.

Colin sat back in his chair. So Maiv was
right. They were all supposed to run away.
And drive to the river in his sketchy white van.
In Colin's head, alarm bells were screaming.
Trap. It had to be. Just as Maiv suspected, the
Benefactor planned to kill them tonight.

It was up to the four of them to make sure
that plan failed.

* * * * *

Colin went to the bathroom in the library,
where he figured the Benefactor's spies couldn't
see him. Carefully, he opened the envelope for
James. What he read was almost as chilling as
his own tasks.

James was supposed to break into
SolarStar—into the office of Jennifer
McKnight—and steal a file called *EarthWatch
Project Proposal.* That was probably the same
proposal Colin had heard Jennifer McKnight
talking about on Monday afternoon. *We only*

have one printout of the proposal, she'd said. *Should I just keep it in my file cabinet?* Colin wondered if the bug he'd had in his pocket had picked up those words. If so, he'd been more useful to the Benefactor than he'd realized.

They were also in a lot more trouble than he'd realized. James was about to steal something, and they were all going to get framed for it. Of course, they were also all going to be dead.

We'll see about that. Gritting his teeth, Colin put the letter back in the envelope.

He went back out to the computer terminals and emailed Maiv to tell her about his last three tasks. He ended the message by saying, *I agree that we have to play along until the last possible minute. But once we're all together in the van, I think we should go rogue. Drive somewhere far away from the river, give the Benefactor the slip, and then come up with a plan to take them down.*

He sent Ana a shorter email, giving her the same gist. By the time he'd grabbed some lunch from a nearby coffee shop and returned to the computers again, Maiv had responded. *My thoughts exactly.*

CHAPTER 16

Back at the motel, Colin found his mom sitting on the bed, staring off into space. Danni was pacing and frowning at her phone. Then she looked up and aimed the frown at Colin. "Decided to join us for a while?"

Colin fought back the urge to tell them everything. He couldn't. It would only put them in more danger. For all he knew, the Benefactor had bugged this motel room somehow. Instead he'd say the words he'd been turning over in his head all day.

He walked over to the bed and sat down next to his mom.

"I'm really sorry about the way I keep disappearing. I promise, I don't like it any more than you do. But things are going to be . . . weird for a while. I'm doing my best to work it out."

His mom kept staring off into space.

Danni crossed her arms. "Something serious is going on with you, brother, isn't it? You've got to level with us here."

"I just did."

"Yeah, like that little speech was supposed to make us less worried?"

Colin looked at Danni—at the healing black eye and the determined, defiantly honest face behind it. "I love you, Danni."

Danni threw up her hands in disgust. "Well, that didn't help at all. Now I'm terrified."

She stormed over to the door. "I'm going out for groceries, Mom. Back in twenty." Colin closed his eyes and hoped it wouldn't be the last time he saw his sister.

* * * * *

Colin went into the bathroom and took a deep breath. He couldn't believe he was doing this.

Leaving his mom right now, leaving Danni, when their business was about to go under, when he'd let them down in so many ways . . . But he had no choice.

He tore a few pages out of Maiv's tiny notebook and started writing. He had to finish this up. It was his fault the business had burned. It was up to him to fix it. He put the letter under the towels that sat above the toilet. That way no one would see it right away.

Coming out of the bathroom, he said, "I'm going out again for a while, Mom." She smiled at him—a faraway, sad smile. "OK, honey."

With one last look at her, he left.

He'd be back. And they would rebuild the store. And he'd make sure Danni could have the surgery. And they'd forgive him, once they knew the whole story. They'd understand.

Tears streamed down his face as he walked down the motel hallway.

CHAPTER 17

Downtown was eerie in the middle of the night. Colin walked toward James, who was standing in front of SolarStar's building, looking nervous. Colin desperately wanted to say something to him. But he couldn't risk it. The Benefactor might have cameras or spies nearby. Instead he brushed past James, bumping into him slightly, and slipped the enveloped into James's pocket. "Sorry," he muttered and kept walking.

He circled the block and came back around to the van to wait for the others. He got into the driver's seat and leaned back.

Suddenly, the passenger door flew open. Colin screamed.

It was Maiv.

And she was trying hard not to laugh.

Colin started laughing too. "I mean, can you blame me for being a little jumpy?"

Maiv climbed in and stowed her backpack under the front seat. "It's nice to meet you. I'm Maiv." She looked at Colin with big eyes, and he understood. The van was probably bugged. The Benefactor couldn't find out that they'd met already.

He cleared his throat. "Colin."

Then Ana's face appeared in the passenger window. Maiv flinched in surprise, which made Colin want to smile. He wasn't the only one on edge.

Maiv opened the door and put her finger to her lips. Ana nodded knowingly. "Is this the van I'm supposed to get in?"

"Yes," said Colin. "I'm supposed to pick up three people."

Maiv stepped out of the van. "I need to stretch my legs."

Brilliant. "Me too," said Colin.

The three of them walked about ten feet away from the van. Then Ana whispered to Maiv, "So you know who the Benefactor is?"

Colin did a double-take. Maiv had figured it out? And she hadn't told him?

"I suspect I know," said Maiv. "But I need to see how everything plays out tonight. And then we have to find proof."

"Yeah," said Ana. "Do either of you know what James is doing in there?"

"Stealing some sort of file—a project proposal," Colin told her.

"And I'm guessing that file contains a physical copy of the schematics," said Maiv. "The electronic copies are probably ruined by now."

Now Colin was confused again. He'd suspected everything was tied to SolarStar's project with Huffmann Industries. But had Maiv found some actual details about that project? "Now you've lost me. What schematics?"

But Ana wasn't paying attention to him. "You mean they only have one hard copy and one electronic file?" she asked Maiv. "That seems weird."

Maiv shrugged. "This is technology all pretty brand-new and super secret, so I don't think they're sharing it with anyone. Not even over email. Too many security risks."

Colin threw his hands up. "Will someone please tell me what's going on?"

Ana said, "All we know for sure is that James just walked into SolarStar with a gun and instructions to steal something."

Maiv's eyes went wide. "He has a gun?"

And that was when they heard the sirens in the distance.

"Crap," said Colin, "that's probably the police." Icicles shot up his spine, and the sweat started.

"Ana, wait!" Maiv shouted, but Ana was already running toward the SolarStar building.

"Start the van!" Ana called over her shoulder.

Colin put his hands on his head—felt the sweat slide from his skin to his hair. "Should we go after her?"

Maiv's face was pale and her eyes were huge. "No, then we'll *all* get arrested if the police show up before we can get away. Let's just do what Ana asked—get in the van and wait for them to come back."

Colin nodded grimly. "If they come back."

CHAPTER 18

As they headed back toward the van, Colin whispered, "So who is it? Who's the Benefactor?"

"I'll tell you my theory when we're all together," Maiv replied.

"And what about this EarthWatch project thing? Is this the thing that SolarStar and Huffmann Industries are working on together?"

"Shh. Wait here—I'll be right back."

"What? You said we should stay with the van—"

"I just thought of something! Two seconds."

Maiv gestured for him to get into the van. He groaned in frustration as she ran off.

Exactly seventy-eight seconds later—he was

counting in his head—she was back, panting, holding a small, dark, familiar object.

"Don't tell me that's—"

Maiv nodded. "The gun. I saw James earlier, on my way over here. He was throwing something into a garbage can. I didn't think much of it until Ana said she'd given him a gun."

Colin stepped back. "Is it loaded?"

"No. I checked. But it's got James's fingerprints all over it and Ana's."

"And mine," said Colin. "I'm the one who bought it."

Maiv nodded. "So we don't want the police to find it. Not until we can explain all this somehow. Now come on, you were supposed to start the van!"

"I know—it's just creepy sitting in there all by myself." Colin opened the passenger door for her.

"A gentleman, I see," said Maiv with a small smile as she got in. Colin blinked. Did that count as flirting? Or had he imagined it?

No time to think about it now. He got into the driver's seat, started the engine, and rolled down his window so he could hear better. The sirens were very close now. He ran his slick palms along the steering wheel. He didn't want to abandon the other two, but what if he had to? If it was a choice between driving away and going to jail . . .

Suddenly Ana and James appeared, both out of breath.

Colin heard James say, "Whoa. Ana? That's you, right?"

Colin leaned out his open window. "No time, dude. Get in."

It only took another ten seconds to convince James that he could trust the three of them. With James and Ana safely in the back, Colin stepped on the gas.

No one spoke, but he could feel everyone's resolve.

They would find this Benefactor. And they would make him pay.

97

ABOUT THE AUTHOR

Megan Atwood lives and works in
Minneapolis, Minnesota, where she teaches
creative writing at a local college and the Loft
Literary Center. She has an MFA in writing
for children and young adults and was a 2009
Artist Initiative grant recipient through the
Minnesota State Arts Board. She has been
published in literary and academic journals
and has the best cat that has ever lived.